For Gibson

For Dad, Mom, and Alan
— P.Z.

www.enchantedlion.com

First published by Enchanted Lion Books,
248 Creamer Street, Studio 4, Brooklyn, NY 11231

Text copyright © 2021 by Maria Popova
Illustrations copyright © 2021 by Ping Zhu

A CIP record is on file with the Library of Congress

ISBN 978-1-59270-3494

Book design: Jonathan Yamakami
Handlettering: Debbie Millman

Printed in Italy by Società Editoriale Grafiche AZ srl

First Printing

the Snail
with the
Right Heart

a true story

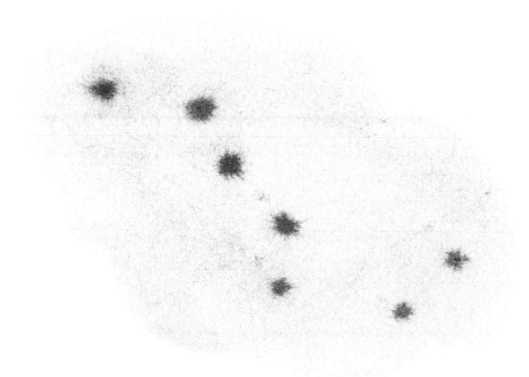

Maria Popova **Ping Zhu**

Enchanted Lion Books
NEW YORK

Long ago, before half the stars that speckle the sky were
born and before the mountains rose reaching for them,
a giant ocean covered the Earth. One day, something strange
happened in the giant ocean — a change so mysterious and
magnificent that it was given a special name: *mutation*.

From this mutation, life was born from non-life, and the
first living creatures — tinier than a grain of sand, tinier
than the tip of the eyelash of a mouse — came into being.

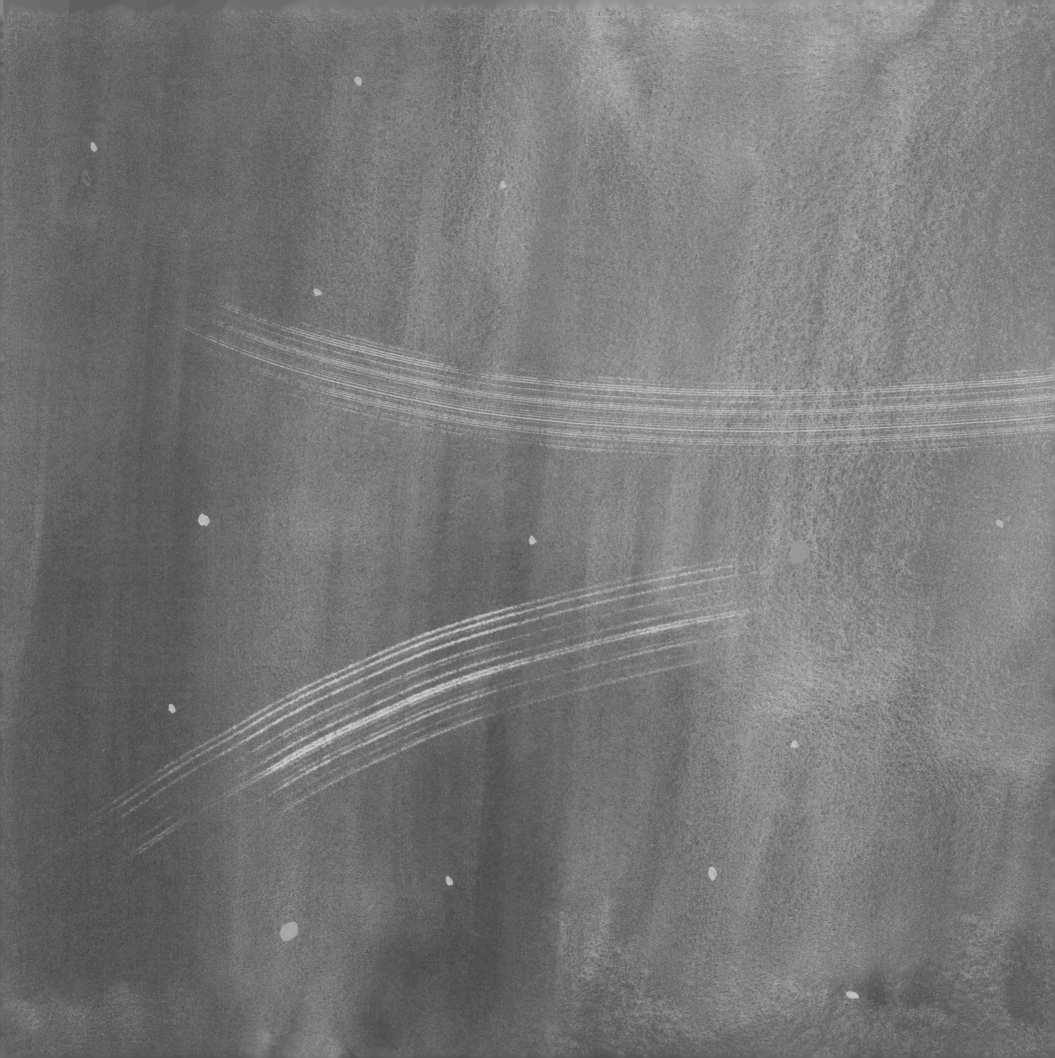

Time tended to them kindly —
they grew bigger and bigger,
curiouser and curiouser.

Soon — which in cosmic time means millions and millions of years — they crawled out of the ocean and onto the land. Not knowing whether they would find a home there, some of these brave early explorers carried their homes on their backs.

And so snails took to the Earth.

Soon — more millions and millions of years later —
humans were walking the Earth alongside them.

One autumn day a cosmic blink ago, a human — a retired scientist from London's Natural History Museum — stopped mid-stride on his walk when he noticed a most unusual garden snail in a pile of compost. It was smaller than the other snails. Its shell was darker than theirs. One of its tentacles had trouble unspooling. And because the snail's tentacles are both its fingers and its eyes, this little snail didn't feel and see the world the way most snails do.

But the strangest thing was something else still: Its shell spiraled not like the shells of common snails but in the opposite direction — it spiraled left instead of right, the same direction the Earth crawls around the Sun.

The old man picked up the little snail tenderly and marveled at it.

It just so happened (isn't chance lovely?) that a few days earlier, he had heard an interview on the radio with a snail researcher named Dr. Angus Davidson. So he decided to send this unusual little snail to Doctor Angus's laboratory. Maybe its strangeness held some beautiful secret waiting to be unlocked.

Carefully, the elder scientist packed
the little snail into a cozy box and
sent it on its way.

When it arrived at the famous snail laboratory, Doctor Angus named it Jeremy, after the British politician Jeremy Corbyn. (Grownups believe that this big round world has sides, so they divide their politics into left and right, like shoes or gloves. Because Jeremy Corbyn belongs to the left, Doctor Angus thought it would be funny to name the little lefty snail after him.)

But although Jeremy the snail was given a boy name, Jeremy the snail was neither a *he* nor a *she* — Jeremy, like all land snails, was both.

Jeremy was a *they*.

One of the wonders of snails is that they can make babies without a mate, because every snail has a body that is both male and female. Such a wondrous body is called a *hermaphrodite*.

If a hermaphrodite makes babies alone, they are almost exactly like their parent. But when two parents make a baby together, the baby is partly like each of them.

And because diversity is always lovelier than sameness, and because it makes communities stronger and better able to adapt to change, snails prefer to make babies in pairs.

Jeremy was so unusual because in their body, a rare recessive gene came abloom — one of Jeremy's great-great-grand-parents must have passed this dormant seed on, until it awakened to make Jeremy's shell coil in the opposite direction.

Jeremy's shell was just the most obvious expression of the mutation, but the entire soft body hidden inside was also a mirror image of almost every other snail's body — a condition known as *situs inversus*, Latin for "inverted internal organs."

This is how it happens: When a snail finds a partner, the two face each other, gently touching tentacles to see if they like each other. And if they do, they glide their bodies alongside one another in a slow double embrace, until their baby-making parts fit together like puzzle pieces. Then, they gently pierce each other with tiny spears called "love darts," which contain their *genes* — the building blocks of bodies.

Genes are like tiny seeds your parents plant in the garden that becomes your body — your special combination of seeds is what makes your body-garden unlike anyone else's and what makes you you. Genes are how life talks to the future. Your genes decide things like how tall you grow, what color your eyes are, and how your thumbs are shaped.

Many of your gene-seeds come abloom in your own body-garden — you get to see, to *be* the flowers they become. But not every one of your seeds will bloom — some only sprout when they are near other seeds just like them. These shy seeds may lay dormant in the soil and only bloom in generations of gardens down the line — in your children, or your children's children, or your children's children's children. Those seeds are called *recessive genes*.

In his twenty years of working with snails, Doctor Angus had never before seen a lefty. He believes that *situs inversus* is rarer than one in 10,000, probably one in 100,000, possibly even one in a million.

Some humans, too, have such wondrous mirror-image bodies — it is just as rare in us as it is in snails. If you had *situs inversus*, your heart would be on the right side — which is the wrong side, because almost everyone's heart is on the left side.

Jeremy's heart was also on the right-wrong side, as were all his vital body parts — which meant that Jeremy could only do the double-embrace dance with another snail who has *situs inversus*, or else the puzzle pieces wouldn't fit together to make baby snails.

Life can be lonesome when your mate is one in a million. And Doctor Angus didn't want Jeremy to be lonesome. He also knew that if Jeremy had babies with another lefty snail, scientists could study this very rare gene and better understand *situs inversus* not only in snails, but in humans. So, he went on the radio again and made an appeal to the whole world to help find Jeremy a lefty mate.

Moved by Jeremy's story, people far and wide got on their knees amid gardens and grasslands and compost piles, determined to find Jeremy's inverted puzzle piece. Within weeks, not one but two potential mates were found — one by a young Englishwoman who kept snails as pets, and another by a snail farmer in Spain.

The whole round world rejoiced when Lefty, the English snail, and Tomeu, the Spanish snail, were sent to Doctor Angus's lab to meet Jeremy.

But the right heart is as hard to find as it is unpredictable — Lefty and Tomeu puzzle-pieced with each other instead, making babies together.

Jeremy was left alone.

Months passed. Lefty and Tomeu's babies loved climbing on Jeremy's shell to play. Maybe Jeremy could discover a different gladness in being an aunt-uncle.

And then, one day, Tomeu left Lefty to mate with Jeremy.
Left or right, the heart wants what the heart wants.

But before the world could celebrate the long-awaited end to Jeremy's lonesomeness, Jeremy died of old age. They had lived a long life for a snail, but they never got to meet their children — the 56 snails Tomeu delivered.

And Doctor Angus didn't get to study *situs inversus* in this next generation, because none of the babies had left-spiraling shells. The recessive gene that caused the mutation had once again become a dormant seed in the garden of life.

But somewhere,

in some future garden,

it will bloom again.

Somewhere down the 56 lines that begin with Jeremy and Tomeu's babies — maybe one, or ten, or a hundred generations down the line; maybe when some of the stars that speckle the sky are gone and new stars are born — there will be a mini-Jeremy. A strange and lovely little snail with a left-coiling shell and a right heart.

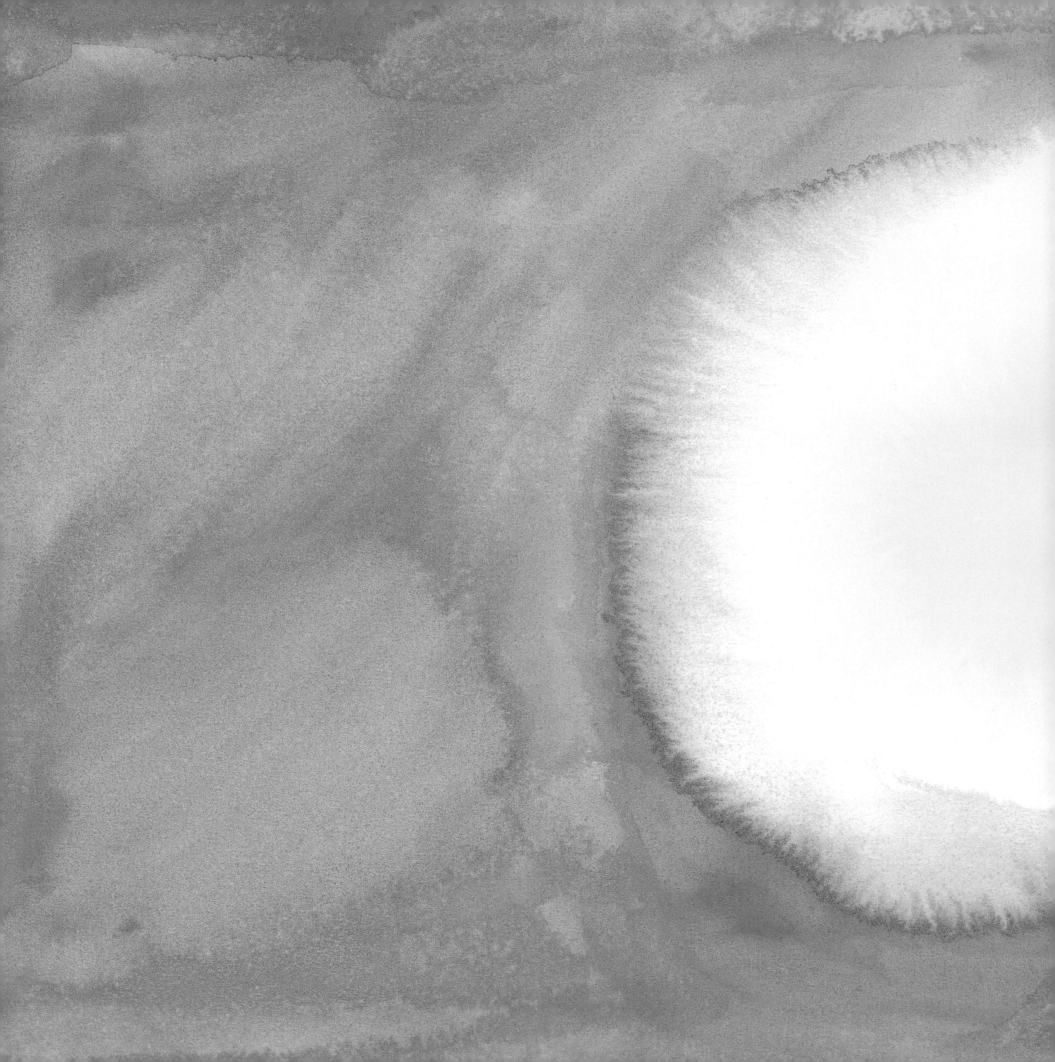